Atlantic Ghosts

Tales of the Haunted Coast

Words and Art by

Bee Stanton

NIMBUS
PUBLISHING
NIMBUS.CA

To my Matt—

a few words in a dedication cannot convey how grateful I am for you.
–BS

Nimbus Publishing Limited
3660 Strawberry Hill St
Halifax, ns B3K 5A9
(902) 455-4286
nimbus.ca

Nimbus Publishing is based in Kjipuktuk, Mi'kma'ki, the traditional territory of the Mi'kmaq People.

Printed and bound in China
Editor & Designer: Whitney Moran
NB1745

Library and Archives Canada Cataloguing in Publication

Title: Atlantic ghosts : tales from the haunted coast / words and art by Bee Stanton.
Names: Stanton, Bee, author, illustrator.
Identifiers: Canadiana 20240359771 | ISBN 9781774713358 (hardcover)
Subjects: LCGFT: Ghost stories. | LCGFT: Short stories.
Classification: LCC PS8637.T3536 A92 2024 | DDC C813/.6—dc23

Nimbus Publishing acknowledges the financial support for its publishing activities from the Government of Canada, the Canada Council for the Arts, and from then Province of Nova Scotia. We are pleased to work in partnership with the Province of Nova Scotia to develop and promote our creative industries for the benefit of all Nova Scotians.

Contents

Introduction 5

The Lady in Blue 7

Emily of Garrison House 9

The Ghost Miners of Bell Island 11

The Fire Ship of Baie des Chaleurs 13

The Hidey-Hinder 15

The Ghost of a Brewmaster 17

The Stewardess of Seal Island 19

Widow's Watch 21

West Point Lightkeep 23

The Guard Dog of Oak Island 25

The Veiled Widow of Christ Church Cathedral 27

Jerome 29

The DeBlois Ghost Train 31

Seminary House of Acadia 33

Fairy Struck 35

The Phantom Oarsman 37

The Grey Lady 39

The Lunenburg Werewolf 41

The Ghosts of Churchill Mansion 43

The Sirens 45

Fresh Paint on Devils Island 47

The Woman in Black 49

A Theatrical Ghost 51

A Fatal Broken Heart 53

Curse of the *Mary Celeste* 55

Works Consulted 56

Introduction

————

Every October since 2018, I have taken part in the monthly drawing challenge known as "Inktober." Each year I stick to a prompt list, usually one I have prepared myself. In 2021, I was inspired by an old W. R. MacAskill photograph that hangs in our home; it features two fishermen in a dory, shrouded in fog and mist, a gentle ripple in the water. The scene is haunting and it captivates me. Staring at that photo one day, I decided the theme for Inktober that year would be "Haunted Maritimes."

Each day I set out to draw a tiny, original pen-and-ink artwork, all of them on 3.5-inch paper, with the image itself sometimes only measuring an inch or two. I scoured as many books and websites as I could find and expanded my list to include all of Atlantic Canada, researching ghost stories of Nova Scotia, Prince Edward Island, New Brunswick, and Newfoundland and Labrador. Some were terrifying, some were heartwarming, all were alluring.

I have many historians and writers to thank for the stories. As folklore often goes, many details remain uncertain, but the stories told well are the ones that live on. To those who tell those tales, I am forever grateful.

The art and stories in this book began as a selection from those original drawings done in October 2021, and include other tales I've come across since. I hope they haunt you and mesmerize you, as they did me, with every stroke of my pen.

The Lady in Blue

Peggys Cove, Nova Scotia

Legend has it that long ago, when a schooner shipwrecked off the central South Shore of Nova Scotia, only one person survived: a woman named Margaret, or, as some called her, "Peggy."

Peggy married a local man and settled in the small fishing village near the wreck. Not long before, she had lost two children in an accident and she still mourned them often. One day while Peggy was grieving her lost children by the sea, her husband attempted to cheer her up by dancing a silly jig on the rocks near the water. Now, as true Nova Scotians know, one must avoid the black rocks if one values one's life. Alas, Peggy's husband was taken by the waves.

Peggy cried for her husband, hoping he would surface, but the sea was wild and there was no sign of him for hours. Overcome with grief, Peggy jumped into the ocean, taking her own life.

To this day, some say Margaret never really left the cove. Visitors to the fishing village of Peggys Cove as well as locals have reported seeing a woman in a blue dress, seemingly distraught, on the black rocks. When they attempt to approach her to help, she jumps and disappears.

There are many versions of the story, but one thing is sure: the legend of Peggy of the Cove has captivated all who've heard it. Especially those haunted by a bone-chilling glimpse of the woman in the blue dress.

Emily of Garrison House

Annapolis Royal, Nova Scotia

In the heart of the small historic town of Annapolis Royal, Nova Scotia, is an inn called Garrison House. Built in 1854 in one of the oldest settlements in North America, formerly known as Port Royal, the building is sure to have some history lurking within it.

It has been said by many a guest and staff member that one particular presence, a rather mischievous one, has made herself known over the years: a playful little girl, known as Emily, who seems to have a special fondness for women. Indeed, any guests who sense her presence are always female, and always staying in one particular room on the top floor. These guests have heard things such as the sound of a child's footsteps running playfully up the stairs, or even the occasional shriek of giggle...when no children are in the building.

If you visit Garrison House one foggy night and hear the laughter of a wee girl, don't be spooked; she means no harm. Just a little fun.

The Ghost Miners of Bell Island

—

Bell Island, Newfoundland and Labrador

The largest island in southeastern Newfoundland and Labrador's Conception Bay, Bell Island claims to be one of North America's most haunted places. With a rich history of mining, and a knack for attracting a wide variety of characters over the years, there is no shortage of folklore.

The coal mines put food on the table for hundreds of families throughout the nineteenth and twentieth centuries in Newfoundland. Day in and day out, the men made their way deep into the windswept rock just west of St. John's.

The mines were no place for the faint of heart. The treacherous nature of the job included cave-ins, falling rocks, and haphazard explosions, taking the lives of countless hard-working men and boys.

And trapping their souls in the depths.

Many claim to see such souls. In fact, several decades ago a family who lived on Bell Island was eating breakfast one Sunday morning next to the kitchen window. The mine, which could be seen in the distance, was closed for the day. When the wee lad at the table asked why the men were just now finishing their shift, his mama told him not to be so foolish, it was Sunday. But when the youngster insisted his parents look, they stopped cold. Sure enough, out from the mine came a line of men, trudging slowly through the foggy morning.

Odd enough for the miners to be working a Sunday, but odder still, when they appeared to be men who'd been killed at work, long ago.

The Fire Ship
of Baie des Chaleurs

In 1501, a Portuguese captain sailed into Chaleur Bay, an arm of the Gulf of St. Lawrence separating New Brunswick and Quebec. The French name, "Baie de Chaleur," translates to "Bay of Warmth."

This was the captain's second trip to the area—but it would be his last. On his previous trip, he'd kidnapped several Indigenous people to sell into slavery; because of this, his return was met by an angry mob seeking vengeance—and vengeance they received. The man was killed and thrown into the sea.

A year later, the captain's brother arrived in search of him. The locals, wanting no relation of such a man near their home again, set the brother's ship afire. It sunk deep into the bay, the crew perishing with it.

Many say the ship still haunts the waters of Chaleur Bay. Hundreds of locals have claimed to witness it. An arc of light appears, taking the form of a three-masted galley ship, its sails and rigging completely engulfed in flames. Some brave schooner captains have even tried to catch it, but like the fog, it slowly fades into the night the closer you get.

The ship is most often spotted before a storm, or on a full moon. Perhaps the Portuguese captain and his brother were cursed, driven mad with lunacy. Cursed to haunt Baie des Chaleurs, paying the eternal price for their cruel and heartless deeds.

The Hidey-Hinder

Dagger Woods, Nova Scotia

On the North Shore of Nova Scotia, there lies a patch of forest and marsh-land known as Dagger Woods.

For the last three hundred years, ever since the area was first settled, it has been haunted by a presence known as the Hidey-Hinder. Some believe it to be a man; others a beast—some even believe it to be both: a man whose darkness so strongly overtook him that only a monster remains.

Those unlucky enough to have encountered the creature describe an inhuman, blood-curdling scream in the distance, which then repeats, each time closer and more deafening. None can clearly describe the Hidey-Hinder's appearance; those who draw close lose their nerve and flee. And of course, some may have gotten a closer look, but were never seen again.

The Ghost of a Brewmaster

In 1820, Alexander Keith, an immigrant from Scotland, opened a brewery in Halifax. Little did he know his brewery would last two hundred years and become an empire.

Keith became a respected fixture in Halifax, and not just for brewing a mean beer. A two-time mayor, he ran the city as well as his business. Respect lasted through the ages, even after the brewery, A. Keith and Son, was sold to rival local company Oland and Son Limited in 1927.

The three-storey sandstone brewery is still a prominent part of downtown Halifax's Historic Waterfront Buildings. Thousands of visitors and staff have walked its halls. A few have even caught a glimpse of Keith himself.

The brewmaster seems to be sticking around his old stomping grounds. Some staff have reported seeing a white-bearded older gentleman roaming the building, perhaps checking in on his brew.

If you're ever in downtown Halifax for a brewery tour, be sure to keep an eye out around every corner. And no worries, Keith's ghost seems friendly enough.

The Stewardess of Seal Island

Seal Island, Nova Scotia

On October 31, 1891, the steamer SS *Ottawa* was en route to Saint John, New Brunswick, from Halifax, Nova Scotia.

It was a dark and stormy night, a southwest gale blowing a heavy head sea all along the coast. As the steamer made its way around the southernmost tip of Nova Scotia, the electric light failed, altering the deviation of the compass. Despite the Seal Island Light clearly visible in the distance, the *Ottawa* ran aground.

The ship struck a rock, took on water, and began to sink. The passengers took to the lifeboats. Aboard one of these boats were three men and one Mrs. Annie Lindsay, the ship's stewardess. In the onset of a rogue wave the lifeboat was overturned, hurling the passengers into the sea and trapping them beneath the boat. Two of the men managed to get to the surface and pulled themselves onto the keel, making it all the more difficult for their companions to surface. As the wave tossed them about, the boat eventually turned upright again. The third man had managed to survive, but Mrs. Lindsay did not.

The men eventually made their way to the shores of Seal Island, the poor stewardess's body in tow. She was buried by the East End church, her grave marked years later.

Locals believe that sometime afterwards, Mrs. Lindsay's coffin was disinterred. The inside of the coffin was covered with scratches resembling claw marks, evidence that Mrs. Lindsay was potentially buried alive.

Legend has it that Annie's spirit roams the island all these years later, haunting all who happen upon her dreaded grave.

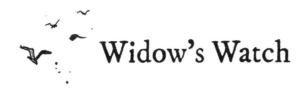

Widow's Watch

Lunenburg, Nova Scotia

Have you ever been to the town of Lunenburg on Nova Scotia's South Shore and admired the grand old architecture? You may have noticed on several homes what is known as the "Lunenburg Bump": a projection built from the centre of the house, over the front door, in a five-sided Scottish style.

The Lunenburg Bump is also known as "The Widow's Watch." You see, in the Age of Sail, this port town (home to the famous *Bluenose* schooner) was bustling with sailors, fishermen, boat builders, and more. While a sailor went off to sea, his wife could often be found in the highest window of their home, anxiously awaiting the return of her beloved.

As you can imagine, the North Atlantic is cold, relentless, and unforgiving. Many a sailor never made it home. And many a widow never gave up.

To this day, if you walk the old streets of Lunenburg some foggy night and seek out a Lunenburg Bump, you just may see a widow in her watch.

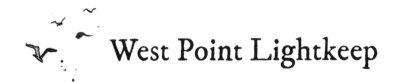

West Point Lightkeep

West Point, Prince Edward Island

On the most western point of Prince Edward Island, a sixty-seven-foot lighthouse stands vigil over the Northumberland Strait and Egmont Bay. In West Point's eighty-eight years as a staffed lighthouse, there were only two keepers. The first was William Anderson MacDonald, serving a whopping fifty years, from 1875 to 1925. Benjamin ("Bennie") MacIsaac took up the torch until 1963, when the light became automated and he was no longer needed; the end of an era.

With both lightkeepers long since passed, and the light left to run on its own, one would think the house and its grounds would be an uneventful place.

Not so.

Many of those who have stayed in the lighthouse and maintained the buildings and grounds claim that a bearded man, not unlike one William Anderson MacDonald, sometimes makes an appearance. He is particularly fond of the bedroom, and often switches the light on, even after it has been turned off, and several times at that.

Automation or not, some lightkeepers never stop keeping a light.

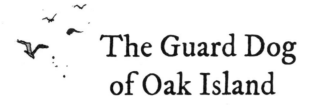

The Guard Dog
of Oak Island

Lunenburg County, Nova Scotia

Oak Island, located a stone's throw from Nova Scotia's South Shore, is riddled with legends, mysteries, and fables aplenty. A literal gold mine of folklore.

The island is a worldwide sensation, as it is believed to be the home of buried treasure. Its infamous Money Pit, a nearly 200-foot-deep manmade shaft on the island's east end, was discovered in 1795, and rumours about what's inside have ranged from Marie Antoinette's long-lost jewels to infamous pirate Captain Kidd's plundered bounty. The island's shores have been searched high and low by countless men and women for centuries. To date, six men have died in the hunt, and legend has it that one more must perish before the treasure is found.

Among the many ghost stories told about Oak Island, that of a huge black dog with glowing red eyes is particularly chilling. Those who have spotted the creature claim it sits watch, often next to a chest. Some have even recalled two knives sitting on top of the chest (if one can believe anyone has ever ventured close enough to see). The beast is thought to be guarding the island's treasure, and cursing anyone who comes close to acquiring it.

Those foolish enough to return to the island after seeing the dog are never heard from again.

The Veiled Widow of Christ Church Cathedral

Fredericton, New Brunswick

Along the Saint John River stands the stately Christ Church Cathedral. Beautiful in its design, and a safe haven for its faithful members, the church serves as a beacon to the community.

And some parishioners of long ago may still roam its grounds.

Several members and passersby have reported spotting a veiled woman in black walking down Church Street, and entering the building through its west doors. Others have spotted her inside the church, either kneeling or seated in prayer.

Many believe the spectre to be the wife of the church's founding bishop, haunting the building and grounds, forever in mourning for her late husband. And while that theory may very well have some truth to it, others take comfort in believing that the woman is simply keeping watch over her flock. The matron was, after all, a very active member of the parish, so much so that she was widely considered to be just as involved as her husband.

Whoever she is, the mystery ghost is certainly an intriguing, and perhaps even reassuring, presence.

Jerome

Digby County, Nova Scotia

Years ago, on a long, skinny peninsula in southwest Nova Scotia, a peculiar event took place. Some young boys were headed to Sandy Cove Beach one morning when next to a big boulder they spotted a man. The boys assumed him dead, and upon closer inspection they were shocked to see both of his legs severed below the knees. The youngsters called for some adults who were equally shocked. As it turned out, the castaway was still alive. They brought him to the nearest shack, stripped his soaking clothes, and warmed him. Once coherent, they questioned the mystery man but couldn't seem to get any answers. In fact, he barely said anything, ever.

News quickly spread of the strange newcomer. The man appeared to be foreign, and no matter how many folks of different languages were brought in, no one could seem to understand him. The closest word they could make out was *Jerome*. And so, this is what the man was called. Though some locals remembered seeing two unfamiliar schooners in the bay the night before he was discovered, no one knew where Jerome had come from.

Jerome was a cold, solitary man. The only time he ever seemed to soften was around the local children. He was sent to the French Shore sometime later, after the suggestion that, by his appearance, he may be Catholic. He lived out the rest of his days in the Acadian community of Meteghan, where he died in 1912, taking with him the mystery of his identity. Some claim to still see Jerome late at night on Sandy Cove Beach, cursed to relive his abandonment on the shores of Fundy Bay.

The DeBlois Ghost Train

Handrahan Crossing, Prince Edward Island

One stormy night in the winter of 1932, a train got stuck on the northern tip of Prince Edward Island. Handrahan Crossing, a place notorious for drifting snow, had claimed the train, while a crew of twenty-four worked tirelessly to dig the engine free.

After hours of digging, and no end in sight to the blizzard, the crew could hear another train approaching, and quickly. Inevitably, the night ended in devastation. The two trains collided with such force that a coach car was split in half. Four people were killed and others were severely injured.

Since that night, and long since the tracks have been gone, a strange phenomenon occurs. On some snowy nights, you may hear a train whistle in the area, where no train ought to be. Some have even reported seeing a ball of light racing their way.

Others have seen a smaller light in the woods, believing it to be the lantern of the engineer, James G. Hessian, still searching for survivors. He was one of the souls who perished that fateful night. Is he bound to search DeBlois forever, tortured by the loss of his crew?

Seminary House of Acadia

Wolfville, Nova Scotia

Founded over 180 years ago, Nova Scotia's Acadia University is no stranger to rich history...and mysterious remnants of such.

On the grounds of this prominent institution, nestled in the fertile Annapolis Valley, there stands a grand building. Acadia Ladies' Seminary was built in 1878 to house a finishing school for female students, as Acadia University was only open to men at that time. But as the building was located in the heart of campus, there was no lack of camaraderie among the students of both schools.

One fateful night, a young woman found herself in a predicament. Pregnant out of wedlock, and unable to bear the embarrassment and scandal her family would face, the poor girl ended her life. She was found hanging in the stairwell of Seminary House.

The building serves as an on-campus residence these days, and is known for strange happenings. Lights flickering on and off, objects moving of their own accord, and strange voices and footsteps in the very stairwell where the tragedy occurred all those years ago.

Does the poor young girl still roam the halls of Seminary House, seeking pardon from her family? Perhaps she is mourning her own life and that of her unborn child. Or perhaps it is only shadows in the night.

Fairy Struck

Newfoundland and Labrador

Many of these tales involve legends of a ghostly nature. While our next bit of lore can't necessarily be called "ghostly," Newfoundland and Labrador are haunted by them all the same.

"Hardtack in ye pocket, sure? Lest ye be fairy struck."

Clear as mud? To many perhaps, but a select few may understand. Those privileged enough to have lived many years on the Rock may recall such advice from their childhood: a reminder to watch out for fairies.

If such a creature evokes a sense of whimsy and images of pixie dust, you likely didn't grow up in rural Newfoundland. These fairies are of a much more sinister nature and are feared by many. Legend has it these fairies roam the woods, terrorizing hikers and hunters, and snatching up children and babies.

Newfoundlanders of old practiced great caution in their daily lives. Carrying bread or hardtack in a pocket, wearing a garment inside-out, or placing a Bible beneath the pillow all provided some form of protection against the little beasts. Many folks also kept an offering of bread and milk outside their door.

While none can prove the existence of such creatures, if you're ever visiting Newfoundland, be sure to stop by a bakery before any long hikes. Lest ye be fairy struck.

The Phantom Oarsman

Sable Island, Nova Scotia

Sable Island is often referred to as "The Graveyard of the Atlantic." Hundreds of ships have perished on its treacherous shoals. So much so that for many years the uninhabited island employed a rescue crew. A few members would stand watch on the sandy island's beaches, awaiting any sign of trouble. Once a vessel appeared to be in distress, the crew of twelve set out into the stormy seas aboard a large dory: one man at the bow with a lantern, ten at the oars, and one at the stern.

One fateful night as the crew rowed hard to a fast-sinking ship, a rogue wave overtook the boat, and one oarsman was claimed by the murky depths. Knowing there was nothing they could do, the crew rowed on into the night, hoping to at least save a few of the souls they'd set out for. And that they did.

A few weeks later, the rescue crew was needed again. They set out, short one man. Through the darkness, one sailor spotted something swimming their way. The crew stopped rowing, speechless, as a man clambered up into the boat, took his place in the empty seat, and began to row. Shocked, but with no time to waste, the men carried on. With the help of their ghostly comrade, they managed to rescue every passenger aboard the ship that night. As they rowed back to shore, the mysterious oarsman stood, tipped his hat, and jumped back into the ocean.

Three more rescues were made that season, and each time the spirit of the lost crewman returned to his spot aboard the boat, only to dive back into his watery grave once the crew's work was done. Legend has it the phantom oarsman can still be seen on stormy nights, swimming the seas around Sable Island, searching for someone to help.

The Grey Lady

Several hundred years ago in one of Canada's oldest townships, a deep-sea fisherman was hired to sail a ship to a foreign post. The fisherman had a wife and a family at home, but on his long journey he found his eye wandering with each port he visited. Loneliness got the best of him and he took a mistress. The young lady grew fond of the fisherman, and begged him to take her with him when it was time to sail back to Port Royal.

Once again, the fisherman couldn't bear the thought of another long stint of loneliness at sea, so he agreed to take his mistress with him. The closer they drew to his home port, the more agitated the fisherman became. He would ignore the woman coldly for hours, and was rude and short with her at the drop of a hat.

The night they sailed up the Annapolis River, ever so close to port, the fisherman anchored the ship. In a whirlwind of panic and guilt, he grabbed his mistress and boarded the gig, heading for the nearest beach, away from the lights of town. The fisherman returned to the ship by himself, his face pale, his eyes dark and cold. The young lady was never seen again.

Legend has it the fisherman's mistress still walks the beaches of the Annapolis River, her long grey dress billowing in the wind. Some say the fisherman killed her; others prefer to believe that his heart softened, sparing her life but leaving her to fend for herself. Either way, The Grey Lady's presence around Old Port Royal is assuredly chilling.

The Lunenburg Werewolf

Lunenburg, Nova Scotia

I n 1700s Lunenburg, there lived a young couple just outside of town. A German fellow, Hans, had married an Acadian woman called Nanette from the Cornwallis Valley (now known as the Annapolis Valley). They appeared to live a happy life until their first child was born.

Hans was known to have a temper, and it seemed he was jealous of the child receiving all of his wife's attention. He began to sleep separately from his wife and even ventured out into the night on a regular basis.

At the same time, many reports of an unknown beast were going around town. Farmers were losing lambs or calves, and descriptions of the creature were nothing short of terrifying. Accounts of howling were reported. Many brushed it off as the cries of coyotes, but those who heard it believed it to be a cursed creature.

One day after berry picking, Hans's wife returned to find neither her husband nor their child at home. That evening, when they still hadn't returned, she sent out a search party. What they found chilled the entire town to their bones. The baby was dead, and with it was Hans, distressed and feral...and covered in blood.

The young man was sentenced to hang, but managed to take his own life in his cell just days before. The circumstances of the suicide were gruesome. Young Hans appeared to have ripped at his veins with his own teeth.

Could Hans have been the foul beast that prowled the streets of Lunenburg, his ferocity so unchecked he would turn on his own child? Local stories still told to this day would lead one to believe the cursed creature was a werewolf, a chilling thought for quaint little Lunenburg.

The Ghosts of Churchill Mansion

I n 1890, Aaron Flint Churchill, a wealthy sea captain, built himself an impressive estate. Overlooking Darlings Lake in the port town of Yarmouth, Nova Scotia, the home was built as a summer residence for Churchill, his wife, and their niece Lottie.

Several stories were rumoured of the home, as many rural areas often speculate the goings-on of their rich neighbours. One quite chilling story suggested that Lottie was preyed upon by one of the servants. One night she'd had enough. In self-defence, she killed the servant, and the family covered it up. It was later rumoured that Lottie was driven mad with the memory of that night, and put in a psychiatric hospital.

Lottie and Aaron and his wife are still said to roam the halls of the former Churchill Mansion, now an inn. Some have reported seeing a chair rocking...with no one in it. Mrs. Churchill was known to sit in the chair for hours on end, rocking, awaiting her husband's return from sea. Many guests who stay in Aaron Churchill's former room sense his presence in their dreams. There are others who recall a ghastly stain on the floor where the servant was allegedly killed. The stain has been removed several times, and even the floorboards replaced, only to have the relentless mark return.

Perhaps Mrs. Churchill has returned to her rocking chair, forever waiting and watching for her beloved. Or maybe she sleeps in his room at night, dreaming of him. And Lottie, poor Lottie. Forever cursed to relive the night that would soon drive her mad.

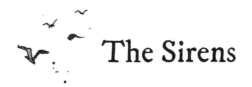

The Sirens

This legend is not specific to the eastern seaboard, but rather the seven seas. For centuries, seafaring men and women have told these tales around the fire by night, or to their little ones, starry-eyed at bedtime: the alluring lore of the Siren.

Some refer to the creatures as merfolk, or mermaids specifically. As these hybrids are described, the torso is often of a woman, and a beautiful one at that, with a large fish-like tail.

In many stories these lovely beings are just that, lovely. But in the more sinister accounts, they are not a creature you want to encounter. Indeed, as the lore goes, when sailors are far from home in their sail, sick with scurvy or aimlessly adrift in the doldrums, there they may find the Siren.

One by one the Sirens call, their captivating song an irresistible lure. And such beauty as well! But what lurks beneath is nothing but evil.

Legend has it many a sailor has lost his nerve—and eventually, his very life— succumbing to the Siren's song. Once she has him in her grasp, down, down, down to the murky depths she takes him. Never to breathe the surface air again.

Fresh Paint on Devils Island

Halifax Harbour, Nova Scotia

There is a tiny windswept island in the mouth of Halifax Harbour. Now abandoned with nothing but a mere shell of the old lighthouse, spirits of old abound.

With a history of shipwrecks before a light was erected, and its ominous name, Devils Island has been labelled cold and unfriendly by those brave enough to visit.

A house on the island known for strange happenings was once inhabited by Henry Henneberry. Henry set out to go fishing one morning and later that day his wife heard him return, his rubber boots a familiar sound. She had been painting the kitchen floor all day and worried it was still wet; she went to let him know. He was nowhere to be found, but sure enough, his boots had left footprints in the wet paint.

It turns out Henry had drowned that day, at the very moment his wife heard him moving noisily about the kitchen. A friendly ghost bidding his love farewell.

The Woman in Black

Wood Island, New Brunswick

On a small island off another island off the southern shores of New Brunswick, you'll find Wood Island. Off Grand Manan, surrounded by the Bay of Fundy, the island was once home to hundreds of families, many of them seafarers.

The island has been barren of full-time inhabitants for many years now. Though the few remaining summer dwellers and visitors know the ever-present haunting feeling instilled by a short strip of road called Ghost Alley.

Many have reported seeing a tall, stately woman walking the old road, dressed head-to-toe in black. When they try to approach her, she turns abruptly and walks effortlessly through anything in her path. Looking away, even for a second, ensures her disappearance.

Legend has it The Woman in Black is a widow, mourning her husband lost at sea. Roaming the island, destined to haunt her shores and Ghost Alley forever.

A Theatrical Ghost

Georgetown, Prince Edward Island

While many Atlantic ghosts are known to haunt pubs, docks, and other port establishments, some seem to have finer tastes. One such spectre has claimed a seat in a prominent theatre on Prince Edward Island.

Kings Playhouse is rich with history, being the country's longest-running theatre. Built in 1887, it has hosted many a performer through the years. Tragically, the playhouse was lost in a fire in 1983, but was quickly rebuilt the following year. And though the original building is gone, spirits of old seem to linger.

Over time, bizarre events in and around the playhouse have been reported by staff, patrons, and even performers. Doors swinging open inexplicably, lights flickering on and off, disembodied voices; one singer walked off stage mid-performance, rattled by incessant whispering in her ear.

Eventually staff members reserved a seat for their resident phantom, nicknaming him "Captain George." It is said that if some unsuspecting soul sits in his seat, the Captain will be sure to express his disapproval. This typically results in the malfunction of lights and equipment, much to the dismay of cast and crew.

Many have debated as to who the ghost could be. The playhouse was built over a graveyard of sailors, and he could very well be the spirit of one such soul buried there long ago.

While Captain George's identity remains uncertain, his passion for theatrics is irrefutable.

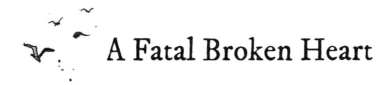

A Fatal Broken Heart

Lunenburg, Nova Scotia

In Lunenburg's Hillcrest Cemetery lies the body of Sophia McLachlan. Her grave is adorned with a wrought iron enclosure, featuring an ornament resembling a broken heart. The fourteen-year-old did die, after all, of a broken heart.

Sophia was apprenticing under a Mrs. Trask, the local dressmaker in Lunenburg. The seamstress often left Sophia to lock up for the evening while she ran errands. One particular night, a sum of ten dollars went missing from the shop. Mrs. Trask immediately accused Sophia of taking the money, and though she denied it, the entire town—including Sophia's own mother—refused to believe her plea. Gossip spread like wildfire, and in no time, Sophia was known as a thief.

Still in mourning from the recent loss of her sisters, Sophia's emotional state couldn't bear any more pain. She quickly took ill, becoming bedridden. Doctors couldn't explain her condition, other than that she was surely dying.

Before Sophia passed, she left a letter for her accuser, insisting her innocence.

Not long after Sophia's death, Mrs. Trask discovered the true thief: her own son, Charles. One can only imagine the guilt that swept through Lunenburg.

The coroner's report concluded the cause of the young girl's death to be "Paralysis of the heart, brought on by extreme agitation and peculiar circumstances."

Sophia McLachlan did indeed die of a broken heart.

To this day, residents of Lunenburg occasionally witness three little girls playing in the cemetery, or hear the laughter of children when none are anywhere to be seen.

A sweet reunion with her beloved sisters to mend her broken heart.

Curse of the *Mary Celeste*

Azores, Portugal, via Nova Scotia

In November 1872, the *Mary Celeste*, a Nova Scotia–built brigantine, set sail for Genoa, Italy, from New York. The crew of ten had no idea the voyage would be their last.

About a month into the trip, British brigantine *Dei Gratia* crossed paths with a ship sailing recklessly about 400 nautical miles off Azores, Portugal. Growing concerned about the ship's strange movements, Captain David Morehouse decided to investigate further. The captain recognized the ship as the *Mary Celeste*, which had left New York Harbor eight days before his own, and sent two sailors to board the vessel.

No one was on board. The sails and rigging were partially torn and charts were strewn about the cabin, but the ship appeared to be seaworthy, and its six months' worth of food and drinking water remained. The hold had about three feet of water, and one lifeboat was missing. But all the crew's personal belongings were undisturbed and the ship's cargo of denatured alcohol was fully intact.

The crew of the *Mary Celeste* was never seen or heard from again.

This is a true story. And while many theories have been presented, from pirates to sea monsters, none can fully explain what happened.

Many believed the ship herself to be cursed, with her troublesome slew of misfortunes. The ship's first captain contracted a fatal bout of pneumonia on its maiden voyage, and the ship itself had been damaged countless times.

The *Mary Celeste* continued to sail under numerous hapless owners and captains, until her final owner wrecked her in 1885 on a reef off Haiti.

Works Consulted

The nature of folklore, typically oral stories passed down over generations and changed in the retelling, make it difficult to trace its origins, However, the author is grateful to the following sources for providing reference material, as well as the locals from several communities who provided stories first-hand.

The Lady in Blue
- *This is Peggy's Cove* by William deGarthe, Read Books, 2010.
- "The True Story of Peggy of the Cove," *Discover Halifax*, September 17, 2016. discoverhalifaxns.com/things-to-do/outdoor-activities/the-story-of-peggy-of-the-cove/

Emily of Garrison House
- "Haunted Annapolis Royal" by Patricia Lonergan, *Annapolis Royal Spectator*.

The Ghost Miners of Bell Island
- "One of the most haunted places in North America, Newfoundland and Labrador has many stories to share" by Krystyn Decker, *The Newfoundland Herald*, February 20, 2018. nfldherald.com/ghost-islands

The Fire Ship of Baie des Chaleurs
- "Fireship of Baie des Chaleurs," *Myth and Folklore Wiki*. Accessed September 2021. mythus.fandom.com/wiki/Fireship_of_Baie_des_Chaleurs

The Hidey-Hinder
- "Dark Sentiments 2011–Day 3, Dagger Woods," *Large Fierce Mammal* blog, published October 3, 2011. Accessed October 2021. randywhynacht.ca/dark-sentiments-2011-day-3/

The Stewardess of Seal Island
- "The Ghost of Seal Island," Nova Scotia Ghost Stories, Folklore, and Legends, *Caretakers Paranormal* blog. Accessed September 2021.
- *Where the Ghosts Are* by Steve Vernon, Halifax, NS: Nimbus Publishing Ltd., 2018.

Widow's Watch
- Lunenburg Ghost Tour Walk, October 2021.

West Point Lightkeep
- "'Chills up your spine': Are old lighthouse keepers haunting West Point?" by Nancy Russell, *CBC News*, October 28, 2017. Accessed September 2021.

The Guard Dog of Oak Island
- *Secret Treasure of Oak Island: The Amazing True Story of a Centuries-Old Treasure Hunt* by D'Arcy O'Connor. Guilford, CT: Lyons Press, 2004.

The Veiled Widow of Christ Church Cathedral
- "The Haunting of Christ Church Cathedral" *Bouncing Pink Ball* blog. Accessed October 24, 2009. bouncingpinkball.wordpress.com/2009/10/24/the-haunting-of-christ-church-cathedral/
- "Christ Church Cathedral," *Haunted Places*. Accessed September 2023. hauntedplaces.org/item/christ-church-cathedral

Jerome
- *Jerome: Solving the Mystery of Nova Scotia's Silent Castaway* by Fraser Mooney Jr. Halifax, NS: Nimbus Publishing, 2008.

The DeBlois Ghost Train
- "Spooky P.E.I.: The phantom ship, mysterious bell ringers and a haunted train track" by Nancy Russell, *CBC News: PEI*, October 30, 2016.

Seminary House of Acadia
- "'The Seminary House's ghostly resident: Nova Scotia Ghost Stories, Folklore and Legends." *Caretakers Paranormal* blog. Accessed June 2, 2021. caretakersparanormalinvestigations.blogspot.com/2018/05/the-seminary-house-ghostly-resident-acadia.html

Fairy Struck
- *Encyclopedia of Newfoundland and Labrador*, volume 2 [Extract: letter F] Memorial University of Newfoundland - Digital Archives Initiative. Accessed April 2024. collections.mun.ca/digital/collection/cns_enl/id/3317

The Phantom Oarsman
- *Haunted Harbours: Ghost Stories from Old Nova Scotia* by Steve Vernon, Halifax, NS: Nimbus Publishing, 2006.

The Lunenburg Werewolf
- "The Lunenburg Nova Scotia Werewolf," *Phantomsandmonsters.com*, account originally written by Theodore Hennigar, published in the *Progress Enterprise*, April 12, 1963.

The Ghosts of Churchill Mansion
- "The Haunted Mansion of Yarmouth" by Paul Andrew Kimball, *View 902*, February 14, 2016. view902.com/the-haunted-mansion-of-yarmouth

Fresh Paint on Devils Island
- *Bluenose Ghosts* by Helen Creighton, Halifax, NS: Nimbus Publishing, 2009.

A Theatrical Ghost
- "Captain George, the Playhouse ghost turns up at recent wedding uninvited and unannounced," *The Eastern Graphic*, May 27. 2014. peicanada.com/eastern_graphic/news/captain-george-the-playhouse-ghost-turns-up-at-recent-wedding-uninvited-and-unannounced/article_04d58f17-29df-5541-bbd2-7844612d547f.html

A Fatal Broken Heart
- Lunenburg Ghost Tour Walk, October 2021.
- "Haunted Lunenburg—Sophia's Story," *Caretakers Paranormal* blog. Accessed October 2021.

Curse of the Mary Celeste
- "Mary Celeste," *Encyclopedia Britannica*. Accessed April 2024. britannica.com/topic/Mary-Celeste
- "Abandoned Ship: The Mary Celeste" by Jess Blumberg. *Smithsonian* magazine, November 2007. Accessed April 2024. smithsonianmag.com/history/abandoned-ship-the-mary-celeste-174488104/